THE SECRET OF THE GIFTS

A Story for Old & Young

THE SECRET OF THE GIFTS

PAUL FLUCKE

Illustrated by Craig Yoe

INTERVARSITY PRESS
DOWNERS GROVE, ILLINOIS 60515

Text © 1982 by Paul Flucke

Illustrations © 1992 by Craig Yoe

Originally published in The Other Side Magazine, December 1982.

InterVarsity Press is the book-publishing division of InterVarsity Christian Fellowship, a student movement active on campus at hundreds of universities, colleges and schools of nursing in the United States of America, and a member movement of the International Fellowship of Evangelical Students. For information about local and regional activities, write Public Relations Dept., InterVarsity Christian Fellowship, 6400 Schroeder Rd., P.O. Box 7895, Madison, WI 53707-7895.

Cover illustration: Craig Yoe

ISBN 0-8308-1841-3

Printed in Mexico

Library of Congress Cataloging-in-Publication Data

Flucke, Paul.
    The secret of the gifts: a story for old and young/ by Paul
Flucke; illustrated by Craig Yoe.
        p.   cm.
    "Originally published in The other side magazine, December 1982"—
T.p. verso.
    Summary: As Gaspar, Melchior, and Balthasar arrive at the stable
to present their gifts of gold, frankincense, and myrrh to the
newborn king, something incredible and wondrous happens, and the
reader learns the secret behind each gift.
    ISBN 0-8308-1841-3
    [1. Magi—Fiction.   2. Christmas—Fiction.]   I. Title.
PZ7.F673Se   1992
[Fic]—dc20
                                        92-5679
                                            CIP
                                            AC

15	14	13	12	11	10	9	8	7	6	5	4	3	2	1
04	03	02	01	00	99	98	97	96	95	94	93	92		

HE STORY HAS BEEN TOLD for centuries now. The story of Gaspar, Melchior and Balthasar, and the gifts they brought to the newborn king. And of how they saw the star and followed it for weeks across mountain and valley and desert. In stately procession on their swaying beasts, they came and placed their treasures at the feet of the infant Savior.

And what *were* their gifts? Ah, you say, everyone knows that. They brought gold, frankincense and myrrh. So, since the earliest days, the story has been told.

But there you are wrong. The story is incomplete. You see, the story was told by those who had seen the wise men on their journey. And by those who stood by in wonderment as the wise men dismounted from their weary camels and strode to the door of the rude stable. They watched as the wise men held their jeweled caskets high before them. That much the world saw. And so the story has been told.

But that is not the whole story. And if you listen very carefully and very quietly, you shall hear the rest of it. You shall hear what happened when the wise men entered the stable. And you shall learn the secret of the gifts.

———————————

GASPAR

HE FIRST OF THE THREE visitors to approach the stable was Gaspar. His cloak was of the finest velvet, trimmed with flawless fur. At his waist and throat were clusters of gems, for Gaspar was a wealthy man.

Those who watched saw only that he paused at the stable door. "He prays," they whispered to one another as they saw Gaspar's lips move. But they were mistaken. They could not see that it was the Angel Gabriel, guarding the holy place, before whom Gaspar stopped.

"And who are you?" Gabriel asked in a voice that was firm but not unkind.

"I am Gaspar, and I come to worship the king," he replied.

"All who enter here must bring a gift," said Gabriel. "Have you a gift?"

"Indeed I have," said Gaspar, and he held aloft a finely wrought box. It was small, yet so heavy that his arms could hardly raise it. "I have brought bars of the purest gold."

"Your gift," said Gabriel somberly, "must be the essence of yourself. It must be something precious to your soul."

"Such have I brought," answered Gaspar confidently, the hint of a smile upon his lips.

"So shall it be," said Gabriel. And he too smiled as he held the door for Gaspar to enter.

* * *

And there, before the rough board wall of the stable, lay the king he had traveled so far to see. The light of the lamp fell across the tiny face and glinted back from the dark, bright eyes. In the shadows sat the parents, motionless and silent. And beyond them, Gaspar sensed the presence of the sheep and oxen who stood their reverent watch.

Gaspar advanced a step and then another. He was just about to kneel and lay his gold before the child

when he stopped and stood erect. There in his out-stretched hands lay not gold but a hammer. Its scarred and blackened head was larger than a man's fist. And its handle was of sinewy wood as long as a man's forearm.

"But, but—" Gaspar stammered as he stared, dumbfounded, at the heavy tool. And then softly, from behind him, he heard the voice of Gabriel.

"So shall it be, and so it is," said the angel. "You have brought the essence of yourself."

Gaspar turned indignantly. "A hammer? What foul magic is this?"

"None but the magic of truth," replied Gabriel. "What you hold in your hands is the hammer of your greed. You have used it to pound wealth from those who labor so that you may live in luxury. You have used it to build a mansion for yourself while others dwell in hovels. You have raised it against friends and made them into enemies—and against enemies to destroy them."

And suddenly Gaspar knew the truth. Bowed with shame, he turned toward the door to leave.

But Gabriel blocked his way. "No, no," he said, "you have not offered your gift."

"Give *this?*" Gaspar blurted in horror, looking at the hammer. "I cannot give this to a king!"

"But you must," Gabriel replied. "That is why you

came. And you cannot take it back with you. It is too heavy. You have carried it for many years, and even now your arms ache with its weight. You must leave it here, or it will destroy you."

And once again, Gaspar knew that the angel spoke the truth. But still he protested. "The hammer is too heavy," he said. "Why, the child cannot lift it."

"He is the only one who can," replied the angel.

"But it is dangerous. He might bruise his hands or feet."

"That worry," said Gabriel, "you must leave to heaven. The hammer shall find its place."

Slowly Gaspar turned to where the Christ child lay. And slowly he placed the ugly hammer at the baby's feet. Then he rose and turned to the door, pausing only for an instant to look back at the tiny Savior before he rushed outside.

The waiting world saw only the smile that wreathed Gaspar's face as he emerged from the stable. His hands were raised, as though the wings of angels graced his fingers. That much the world saw, and so the story is told.

MELCHIOR

EXT TO STEP TO THE DOOR of the
stable was Melchior, the learned Melchior. He was
not so resplendent as Gaspar for he wore the darker
robes of the scholar. But the length of his beard and
the furrows in his brow bespoke one who had lived
long with the wisdom of the ages. A hush fell over
the onlookers as he too paused before the door. But
only Melchior could see the angel who stood guard.
Only Melchior could hear him speak.

"What have you brought?" asked Gabriel.

And Melchior replied, "I bring frankincense, the
fragrance of hidden lands and bygone days."

"Your gift," cautioned Gabriel as he had done before, "must be something precious to your soul."

"Of course it is," retorted Melchior.

"Then enter, and we shall see." And Gabriel
opened the door.

* * *

Melchior stood breathless before the scene within.
In all his many years of searching for elusive Truth,
he had never sensed such a presence as this. He
knelt reverently. And from beneath his robe he with-
drew the silver flask of precious ointment.

But then he drew back and stared. The vessel in his hand was not silver at all. It was common clay, rough and stained as might be found in the humblest cupboard. Aghast, he pulled the stopper from its mouth and sniffed the contents. Then he leapt to his feet only to face the angel at the door.

"I have been tricked," he said, spitting the words with fury. "This is not the frankincense I brought!"

"What is it, then?" asked Gabriel.

"It is vinegar!" Melchior snarled as though it were a curse.

"So shall it be, and so it is," said Gabriel. "You have brought what you are made of."

"You are an angel of fools," Melchior snorted.

But Gabriel went on. "You bring the bitterness of your heart, the soured wine of a life turned grim with jealousy and hate. You have carried within you too long the memory of old hurts. You have hoarded your resentments and breathed on sparks of anger until they have become as embers smoldering within you. You have sought for knowledge. But you have filled your life with poison."

As he heard these words, Melchior's shoulders drooped. He turned his face away from Gabriel and fumbled with his robe, as though to hide the earthen jar. Silently he sidled toward the door.

Gabriel smiled gently and placed his hand on

Melchior's arm. "Wait," he said. "You must leave your gift."

Melchior sighed with a pain that came from deep within him. "How I wish I could! How long have I yearned to empty my soul of its bitterness. You have spoken the truth, my friend. But I cannot leave it here! Not here, at the feet of love and innocence."

"But you can," said Gabriel. "And you must, if you would be clean. This is the only place you *can* leave it."

"But this is vile and bitter stuff," Melchior protested. "What if the child should touch it to his lips?"

"You must leave that worry to heaven," Gabriel replied. "There is a use even for vinegar."

So Melchior placed his gift before the Savior. And they say that when he came out of the stable, his eyes shone with the clearest light of heaven's truth. His skin was as smooth as a youth's as he lifted his face to gaze on horizons he had never seen before. And in that, at least, the story is correct.

BALTHASAR

HERE WAS YET ONE MORE visitor to make his offering. He strode forward now, his back as straight as a tree, shoulders firm as an oaken beam. He walked as one born to command. This was Balthasar, leader of many legions, scourge of walled cities. Before him, as he grasped it by its handle of polished ebony, he carried a brass-bound box.

A murmur ran through those who watched as they saw him hesitate before the door. "Look," they whispered, "even the great Balthasar does obeisance before the king who waits within."

But we know that it was Gabriel who caused the warrior to pause. And we know too the question that he put.

"Have you a gift?"

"Of course," answered Balthasar. "I bring a gift of myrrh, the most precious booty of my boldest conquest. Many have fought and died for centuries for such as this. It is the essence of the rarest herb."

"But is it the essence of yourself?" asked Gabriel.

"It is," replied the general.

"Then come," said the angel, "and we shall see."

Even the fearless Balthasar was not prepared for the wave of awe that struck him as he entered the holy place of the Christ child. He felt a weakness in his knees such as he had never known before. Closing his eyes, he knelt and shuffled forward through the straw in reverence. Then, bowing until his face was near the ground, he slowly released his grip upon the handle of the box and raised his head and opened his eyes.

What lay before him at the baby's feet was his own spear. Its smooth round staff still glistened where the sweat of his palms had moistened it. And the razor edges of its steely tip caught the flickering light of the lamp.

"It cannot be!" Balthasar whispered hoarsely. "Some enemy has cast a spell!"

"That is more true than you know," said Gabriel softly from behind him. "A thousand enemies have cast their spell on you and turned your soul into a spear."

"You speak in riddles," cried Balthasar, turning to face the angel. "I'll teach you not to jest at a time like this." And he raised his fist as if to strike.

Gabriel did not flinch as he continued: "Living only to conquer, you have been conquered. Each battle you win leads you only to another with a foe yet more formidable."

"Do you think I *like* to kill?" demanded Balthasar. "You angels know nothing of this world. I am the defender of my people. Were it not for my spear leading them in battle, we should have been destroyed long ago. Why, even now, the enemy is massing to invade us. As soon as I leave this holy place, I must raise more armies. I must buy more spears to arm them and—"

"More," Gabriel interrupted quietly, "than what?"

"Why, more than we have now. More than our enemies have."

"And what will they do then?" asked the angel softly. "Will your enemies too need more?"

Balthasar heard the angel's words, and they seemed to echo in the deepest places of his soul as though vaguely familiar. Was the question one that he had sometime asked himself? Was it that faintest flicker of doubt, quickly stifled by one who did not dare to doubt?

For a moment, Balthasar hesitated. Then, taking control of himself, he reached down and grasped his spear—and turned toward the door.

"I cannot leave this here," he said. "My people need it. We cannot afford to give it up."

"Are you sure," asked Gabriel, "that you can *afford* to keep it?"

"But our enemies will destroy us if we drop our

spears," Balthasar said impatiently. "We cannot take that risk."

"Yes, it is a *risk,*" Gabriel replied slowly. "But your way is a *certainty*—a certainty of spears."

Once again, Balthasar hesitated. And once again, the sweat of his palm moistened the smooth shaft of the spear. But now the beads stood out on his forehead as well, as the force of Gabriel's words did battle with centuries of warrior instinct.

A long moment passed. Finally Balthasar loosed his grip, and the spear drooped toward the floor. But as he looked at the child at his feet, he whispered anxiously to Gabriel, "But here? Is it safe to leave it here?"

The angel released a long-held breath as he whispered back, "This is the only safe place to leave it."

"But he is a child, and the spear is sharp. It could pierce his flesh."

"That fear you must leave to heaven," Gabriel replied.

And they say that Balthasar went calmly from the stable, his arms hanging gently at his sides. They say that he walked first to Gaspar and Melchior, where they waited, and embraced them as brothers. Then, turning to the others who watched, he went first to one and then to the next, enfolding each in his outstretched arms as one greeting beloved friends whom he has not seen for a very long time.

That, at least, is how the story has always been told. And it is true, as far as it goes. But you have listened well, and now you know the whole of it.

Now you too may kneel before the Christ child to leave at his feet those unseen, secret things that may be left nowhere else but there. And having visited the holy place, you too, like those three visitors of old, may go on your way made new.

But what of their gifts, you ask? What of the hammer and the vinegar and the spear? Well, there is another story about them and how they were seen once more, years later, in fact, on a lonely hill out-side of Jerusalem. But do not worry. That is a burden heaven took upon itself, as only heaven can. And will, even to this very day.

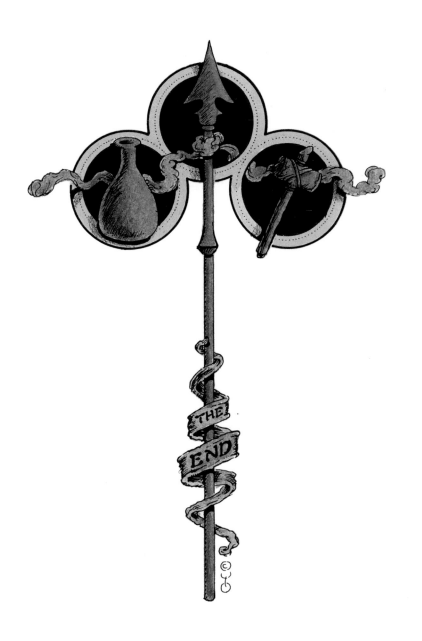

THE END

This edition of *The Secret of the Gifts* is set in 12 point Berkeley and printed on 80# Patina Matte by R. R. Donnelley & Sons Co., Reynosa/ McAllen Division. Color separations are by Computer Color Graphics, Inc. of Hillside, Illinois.